HEAR THE BRANCHES RATTLE

FREDRICK NILES

FEVER GARDEN PUBLISHING

HEAR THE BRANCHES RATTLE

First edition. December 11, 2023.

ISBN: 978-1-950021-16-1

Fever Garden Publishing

Cover design by

TheCoverCollection.com

❀ Created with Vellum

PROLOGUE

Papa is gone but he'll be back.

I don't need to call out to him. Not yet. I'm not lost. I'm not lost because papa knows where I am and he'll be back.

I'm not cold anymore. I was but now I'm not. The sun is warmest in the middle of the opening, away from the dark trees that look like old people's hands. Grandmama had hands like that and she used to hold mine and when she did it felt like I was holding a branch.

Grandmama is gone now up in Heaven but papa said I'd see her again one day if I'm good. So that's why I'm being good and staying put right here in the middle, in the sun.

The sun is a little lower now because night's coming but I'm not worried. I used to be afraid of the dark but not anymore and it doesn't matter because I'll be home soon where it's warm.

I wish I could go and see my mama at home but she's gone too. I'm not sure if I'll see her in Heaven though, even if I'm good, because every time I ask papa he doesn't answer.

He just asks me something else. I hope I see her though so I'll be good just in case.

Okay, I'm going to call out to him now because it's been a long time. It's not that I'm worried but the woods are getting dark now and I don't like walking through them when it's dark, even though I'm not scared of them anymore. I just don't like it.

"*Papa!*"

The sound is funny, like yelling into a blanket. I think it's because of all of the snow on the ground and in the trees which kind of *looks* like a blanket. It's not though or I'd lie down on it and be warm.

"*Papa,*" I call out again. This time it's louder and I try to be brave like he told me to be. I think it's okay if I cry though, because brave people can cry sometimes. My papa's very brave and he cried when we were walking out into the woods today. But I don't think it's because he was afraid. He's never afraid.

I begin to yell for him again but then I don't. Suddenly, I'm afraid, which is okay. Papa also said that sometimes it's okay to be afraid. That there's nothing wrong with it. Which is good because I am afraid.

I hear something. It sounds like the trees are clacking their branches together. Like old people clapping with their bony hands. The sound is getting closer and I'm afraid. I want to run but the woods behind me are dark. The woods all *around* me are dark.

I look up at the sky and can't see the sun anymore. I cry for papa again.

Papa isn't here, but something is.

1

———

It is truly something to watch a whole town die.

The population was always low. People were afraid to have children and the fewer children they had, the more reason the people with children had to be afraid. That's no way to make a town flourish.

I could have left. Hell, I considered it hundreds of times over the years, growing up. As a young man, I dreamt of cities and oceans and places that were green all year round. But even then, I was already stuck here. Chained down by...complicity...

Because you can't go two whole decades without knowing what's happening. You just can't. And how do you bring something like that into the world? How do you go and meet new people in a new area and keep that locked inside of you like some thin, grey devil?

You can't. People have tried but they always return. I was always told that it was something that bonded us, that kept the town alive, and there were times that I thought *bullshit*. But they were right. It did bond us. It did keep us alive, in a way.

When the town itself finally died, it was not with a whimper, I can tell you that much. Some said it was because we got too *high* and *mighty*. That we dared question the old ways. They said that that's why they finally came for us.

Well, I tell you what, you're goddam fucking right I questioned the old ways.

We did what they said. Tina and I followed the rules and only did our business in accordance with the cycle of the moon and we got pregnant just the same.

I can't tell you what it felt like to find out. Like doomed joy. Because we knew. Birthrates were so low at that point I could count the number of kids born that year on my right hand. We knew it would be us eventually. I knew I'd turn that clay pot over one day and find a red flower instead of ash like everyone else.

You lie to yourself though. As the days go on, you think that maybe it *will* be okay. Maybe she *will* make it the full 13 years. 13 random drawings. You invest, even though. Even though you know. The questions and doubts are always pushed off until tomorrow.

That is, until tomorrow doesn't come.

Sometimes I wonder if Tina didn't make the smart choice. When she did it, there weren't any signs. No mood swings, beyond what was normal for us. No slow slide into depression. My guess is, one day she just looked our daughter in the eyes and made a silent decision for herself.

I don't blame her. How could I? If anyone understood, it was me. Alexis was three when it happened, which would have meant ten more years of looking down into her smiling face, full of warmth and future, and wondering if this was the year.

. . .

THEY CAME for us four years after I left Alexis in the woods. I'm not sure why. Maybe they were dying too. Maybe they were starving like we were.

The animals were almost all gone at this point. That's what they ate most of the time, saving the sacrifices for a single day in the dead of winter. After the town died, I still didn't see a deer for six whole years. Sure, the birds and squirrels repopulated quickly, but they were small things. Nothing that size can subsist on rodents and songbirds for very long.

I survived by fishing the river. Still do. Although, sometimes I wonder why I go on. The last member of a dead and forgotten town on the edge of nowhere, loving only memories and the dim image of a time that once was and never will be again.

I'm 53 now. The winters feel colder and the ax feels heavier but I continue on. I can't say why. Maybe there's something inside of me that still believes what I told Alexis all those years ago. That if you're good, you'll go to Heaven.

That was never my bag, really. Tina's mom was the one who believed in it. Maybe not in the Christ god so much as Heaven. A place somewhere far off that was immune to everything that was done here.

Word of the Christ god drifted in here on the tongues of doomed missionaries traveling the wilderness a hundred years ago. They died screaming but somehow their message stuck and existed uneasily alongside the old ways. Never allowed to climb up on top of the gods of the woods but always simmering under the surface.

I wonder what the old gods thought of that. Competition, no doubt, but in some people's case it was sort of an anesthetic. A daydream to keep your eyes off of the horrors all around you.

If there is a Heaven, I will not be going there. Not after everything.

Tina's mom used to tell me that it's not about being good, it's about accepting Jesus into your heart. I never had the courage to ask her how she lived with herself. How she managed to juggle so many gods in her head. I never asked if there was room enough in her heart for Jesus and the ghosts of a hundred children.

Lord knows there isn't in mine.

Yet, if the Christ god ever entered my heart, it would be as a Holy Ghost, for my heart is a home for spirits, dead or otherwise. If it were to enter me as she said, it's hard to imagine it wouldn't be in a rush of fire and fury. I feel like it would utterly destroy me, leaving nothing but ashes and regret.

Regret is all there is now. Not regret for the way things are as much as the way *I* am. The kind of person that hands his daughter over to the slavering jaws of beasts. You may ask yourself why I didn't just tell them to "get fucked" when I drew the red flower. Now, after knowing all that I know, I should have. But it's not so easy.

I remember being ten years old. I remember what they did to those who tried to escape.

THE DAYS ARE GETTING SHORTER NOW. The nights, colder. Winter will find me well-stocked on firewood, food, and oil.

If I ever decide to escape, there is one person who knows I'm here. Paul Fletcher, the bush pilot who used to bring us supplies. I was never sure of his connection to the village, but since the rest of the town was wiped out, he's cut his trips down to once a year.

He lands his float plane on Big Harriet Lake and then

cruises in towards the dock. I'll never forget the look on his face when I told him that the rest were gone. It was emotionless. As if I had just told him a big tree had fallen down in the backyard.

Some day, he will motor on up to the dock and no one will be there to greet him. I don't know how much he knows about the town but I doubt he'll venture in to see if anyone needs help. He'll probably just leave and never come back.

Good riddance.

THE SUN HAS JUST BEGUN to touch the horizon. There's a deer I've been waiting for all afternoon but I don't think she's coming in, even with the big bait pile. She's too wary. Would have to be, I suppose.

I could probably catch her around twilight but I don't think it's worth the risk. Not yet.

I stagger up off the stump I've been sitting on and sling the rifle over my back. I've fired it four times in the last year, each time at an animal I intended to eat. I never missed once, thank God, and the sight is still accurate.

When I get inside, I lean the rifle against the edge of the doorframe and bolt the door. Apparently, there are some towns where everyone leaves theirs unlocked. I can't imagine. A different life. A different world.

One hour later and dinner is done. Mushrooms and venison backstraps. I eat, staring at the wall, trying not to look. Trying not to think about it.

The food is down in an instant and I am unsatisfied. It's dark now. I look toward the window where the curtain is pulled, then to the door and its lock, then to the gun, then back to the wall.

I see my smudged reflection in the blade of the dinner

knife laying on the table. Beard and scraggly hair whiter than the last time I cared to look. An old blotchy scar that stretches from the left side of my forehead down to the nape of my neck. Pinprick pupils swimming in bloodshot milk, their gaze averted just so.

My finger starts tapping on the wooden table where there is a slight divot from this exact habit. Years and years of wear. Not just on the table.

I break, like I always do, hating myself. I drag the chair over to the window and sit down, the wooden legs creaking. I brace myself, breathing in.

You don't have to do this.

The voice of reason in my head must be tired at this point, after being ignored for so many years. Even so, it persists, speaking to some undefinable bit of humanity I'd just as soon leave outside with the wary deer and waiting woods.

I draw back the curtain and there she is.

"Papa."

The first time it happened, I cried so hard I lost my voice. And she sat there, watching through the glass like she is now.

"How was your day?" I ask.

"Good. I saw mama and grandmama."

"Really, what'd you do?"

She shrugs. "Not much. We had a picnic in the clearing. I had jammy bread."

"Jammy bread?" I raise my eyebrows. "What kind of jam?"

"Raspberry. Mama had to pick them very carefully, because of the stickers."

"I bet. Those stickers can be tricky. Did I ever tell you

about the time my friend and I tried racing through the raspberry patch without our shirts on?"

"Yeah, and you came out bloody?" She asks. And at that, something twitches in her face. An almost imperceptible movement that darkens her expression. But then she is back again. Her usual brilliant, beaming self.

I don't know why I do it. Mention the thorns and the scratches and the blood. Maybe it's something deep down in my subconscious looking out for me. Reminding me that this isn't real.

Because it's not.

I remember this for a moment and the illusion is broken. Sadness engulfs me and I try to work my way back into the fantasy. Into forgetfulness.

"Papa, where did you go?"

I am unable to respond to this and she sees it.

"I'm waiting out there for you," she says. Her voice is a little quieter now. More distant. As if she's trying to speak to me from the past. "It's getting *really* cold."

"Colder every day now," I say absently.

She nods and for the first time, I see it. Something in her cheeks and neck. Something that makes her seem...thinner.

Something moves in the corner of my vision and my eyes dart to the mouth of the trail at the back of the yard. There's something there but I can't quite see it.

Then it looks up and my heart leaps into my throat. Yellow eyes, staring in at the cabin. Watching. Assessing. They bob as it walks slowly across the yard. Its form is hunched, bone-thin legs tottering over the rough earth and dried leaves.

Oh no.

It's the doe. She's finally moving in to the bait pile, now

that I'm inside. I could *maybe* open the window and point the gun out but...

Alexis gasps and a massive smile leaps to her face when she sees what I'm looking at. It's as if I've just given her a present. She turns and looks at me, almost as if she's asking permission.

It sees her too and stops, ears up.

Alexis steps away from the window and goes skipping across the yard, the deer bolting into the woods. The last I see of her before letting the curtain fall back into place is the white winter jacket she was wearing the day we walked to the clearing. It disappears into the dark beneath the trees.

I am in Hell.

2

———————

I find the deer the next morning. It made it maybe…two hundred paces into the woods. One of its front legs is twisted out of the socket, its head removed and lying a few paces away.

Little blood on the ground and in the leaves. What's more, is that the animal looks too skinny. Bloodless.

Alexis will look bright as ever tonight, without a trace of that thinness I saw.

I should thank her. The deer is dead and already drained. A part of me wonders if she left it on purpose. And if so, which *part* of her left it? The part of her that's my daughter or the part of her that wants me fed, like the witch in Hansel and Gretel. The part of her that's hungry.

Back at the cabin, I hang the deer upside down by its feet. With its blood gone, it now needs to age and tenderize. There shouldn't be much for bears or scavengers in the area. Just me.

I walk into the woods without realizing where I'm going. I feel like I'm floating and that should be an indication that I'm about to walk into something difficult. That my subconscious is trying to keep me distracted as long as possible.

My feet stop moving and I'm there. The birds are chirping around me. The sun is still climbing. I turn and observe the clearing. Why am I here?

Near the end, when people began wandering off into the woods at night, I wondered if the things that were taking them were more than just animals. They seemed to have a spirit about them. An air that moved the heart and bent the will, almost like hypnosis.

I often wonder if that's why I outlasted them. I never gave in. Not quite. Because while the visits from Alexis were painful and destructive, they were also something like a drip feed into my soul, sustaining me. An anti-venom of sorts. Just enough poison to keep me alive.

In my time on this earth, she was the only one to ever come back. There were stories of such things before, of course, but nothing that more than a handful of people had been around to witness. I'm not sure why the creatures chose her. Why the monsters let her continue to exist as she now does.

Maybe it was one last gambit for their own future. A failed one, ultimately, but worth a shot. Because she lived as they turned to dust. She sustained while they withered.

And now, here we both are. Connected not just by our familial bonds but by the fact that we are each the last of our own kind. Slowly feeding off of each other in ways I'm sure neither of us quite understand.

I turn slowly in the center of the clearing, drinking in the sorrow. The memories. Walking with her in the woods in the time before. Catching a fish from the lake and handing her the rod at the last moment, to let her feel the thrill of the catch on her own. The quiet nights together with her and Tina, playing with her as she crawled over the floor.

The sounds of the day fade to the background as I consider what I'm doing. There is some suggestion in the air that if I finally join Alexis, I will be allowed to slip comfortably into the past. It sounds like a lie but an appealing one nonetheless.

I entertain the idea a few moments longer and then turn back around. There is a revolver back in my room at the house. The whole walk back, I think about using it.

SHE COMES AGAIN THAT NIGHT. A light tapping on the window, I pull back the curtains and there she is, as bright and lively as ever I've seen her.

"I saw you in the woods today, papa."

"Did you?" The question is genuine. I wonder if she knows I was there through some connection I don't quite understand or if she actually saw me there, watching from some dark corner.

She nods her head vigorously. There is a tinge of blue in her cheeks, which makes me instantly want to let her in out of the cold. But no, it's not a problem. She doesn't feel it.

"When are you going to join us?"

"You and mama, you mean?"

"Yeah." She smiles. "We're waiting."

"Why doesn't mama ever join you?" I ask. "Where is she?"

Alexis looks down for a moment, a perfect imitation of feeling uncomfortable.

"She doesn't think you want to see her. She says you're too stubborn. Too selfish."

"Maybe I am," I say. I try to focus more on the low-key

battle of wits rather than the actual words. If I acknowledge what she is actually saying, I know I'm through.

"I don't care about that, papa." She's shaking her head suddenly, as if she's just lost her patience. "I just want us all to be together again."

"Will we?"

"Will we what?"

"Be together again? All of us?"

Her eyes bounce back and forth between mine, confusion plain on her face. She does a good job. Pretending, I mean. Pretending to be her.

It, I think to myself. *It* does a good job.

And suddenly I'm angry. At this charade. At this whole thing. I am disgusted with myself. I think about the stuff in back. It would only take a few moments to get ready. Then everything would be over. No more lies or illusions. Just black and blissful nothingness.

But is it nothingness? I have to ask myself the question because the thing sitting here in front of me is an affront to the notion of the permanence of death. Because Alexis *is* still in there. I have no idea how to get her out but she understands too much about me, about my family, to just be some monster.

Still, I almost do it. I almost end the entire thing. A form of giving up, really. Which was never something I was known for.

But that was then and this is now. I've lived for decades here, alone, slowly poisoning myself with her. Even a stone is worn down by time.

I resist, though. I resist both her solution and mine, choosing instead to prolong this purgatory as I have a thousand times before.

3

———

I dream of the Kristophsons.

Maybe it's less of a dream and more of a photo album of memories seared into my brain. Mr. Kristophson's ashen face as he draws the red flower. Mrs. Kristophson making a noise like a kicked dog. Her screams the next night and the smell of smoke stinging my nostrils.

The feeling of something hot and wet scorching my face and neck.

A few years after, my father told me that he knew they would try to run. Apparently, he and Mr. Kristophson had discussed it on multiple occasions. This sounded like madness to my teenage years. Heresy. It wouldn't be until I had a wife and child of my own that I would come to realize it was a conversation that everyone was having all the time. Perhaps all the way back to the beginning.

Maybe a shadow of doubt and a whisper here and there were permissible. Let the villagers work through the problem. Let them realize that there was no escape. Not really.

Mr. Kristophson took it too far though. He was always

trying to figure out a way to escape. Trying to scheme and work the angles. I remember overhearing him talking with my father once, asking him if he thought it was true that they couldn't travel over running water.

That's how they ended up trying to escape. Mr. Kristophson had stowed a canoe away beneath a brush pile some time before in case the day ever came. The house was watched closely after the drawing but no one but the Kristophson family knew of the tight tunnel that had been dug in the cellar. It was only about two hundred paces long. It let out at the base of a giant fallen cedar tree, its entrance obscured by masses of hanging roots. But that was enough to cover the escape.

To this day, I don't know who tipped the watchers off about the canoe. I do know that there were eyes that watched the family very closely, not all of them human. But in my dreams, I see the firelight reflecting off of my father's eyes. My father, Mr. Kristophson's childhood friend. I see his face shining with tears.

Would I recognize those tears for what they were if things had been different? Would I suspect him now that I knew what guilt looked like as it stared back at me from every reflection?

I don't know if it was him that sentenced them to death but I know it's strange that I lived.

When they dragged the Kristophons to the blackened stakes at the center of town, ripping the child from his mother's arms as they both wailed, all I could think about was the possibility that I was next.

After all, that was the punishment. Run and you damn your whole family and two of your neighbors' children. They were eventually forced to reduce it to one neighbor's child as the population continued to dwindle but at that time it was still two and I was sure I was one of them.

I remember standing there sweating in the town's square, looking up at my mother and father. I remember them shifting nervously as the men in black masks walked towards us. Then I remember relief and dread washing over me simultaneously as two other children were torn from the crowd, arms outstretched. Faces red and streaked with tears.

The five of them were burned there. Mr. and Mrs. Kristophson. Their son, Felix, who I had played with since before I could remember. Tracy from the Westfell household, age seven. Peter from the Grayson household, age three.

We watched as the fire burned, the upper crest of the sun dipping below the tree line in the west just as the skin on their shins started to crackle. Thinking back, the sound of the fat beginning to pop in their legs is the same sound as the rattling of branches behind me.

I'll never forget how the bloody sky at dusk was suddenly blotted out by huge flying shapes. They dipped closer and closer to the flames, their true forms on full display. Translucent icicle-length teeth and leathery wings. Dented-in noses. Ruby eyes.

Each of the five victims was ripped into the air, some dead or unconscious and some awake and screaming. I was close to Mrs. Kristophson when she was snatched, her arms breaking as they were wrenched from the ropes that bound her. She didn't scream. I'm sure she was already dead.

I tried to track her as she disappeared into the sky. I saw her limp and dangling shape as the creature writhed against her. Then the next thing I knew, I was on the ground screaming, my face in agony. The blood, super-heated from the fire, splashing down onto my cheek and neck.

.   .   .

I WAKE UP, my hand darting reflexively beneath my pillow before I know where I am. I feel that heat on my face. That same cloying wetness. It isn't until I'm furiously rubbing it off with the back of my hand that I realize it's my own tears.

The bed creaks beneath me as I try to catch my breath. The moon is full in the sky tonight, its silver rays trying their best to slip in through the cracks in the curtains. The sound of the fire crackling in the pot belly stove sets my teeth on edge and I have to force a wave of nausea down.

"You know why we have to do it, right?"

My father's words echo through my mind, taking me back to the morning a few days after the incident. Before those images in my head were wounds. Before the wound on my face was a scar.

"Yes." I didn't elaborate.

A moment of silence passed as he looked at me, his brow creased with worry.

"Can you explain it to me?" He asked. "In your own words?"

I took a deep breath, the fresh burns stretching painfully beneath the bandage that was covering half of my face.

"Because they'll kill us if we don't."

"Something will always try to kill you, son. That is the way of things. If we didn't have the gods in the woods then it would be something else. Wolves. Bears. Wicked men."

"What keeps us from being wicked?" I asked. I wanted to explain how I felt the other day, watching what happened to those kids. To those families as they were torn from each other. From the world. I wanted to tell him that I had never felt more wicked in my whole life.

"Wickedness," my father's voice hardened. "Wickedness is closing your eyes when you cut someone's throat so you don't have to see them bleed. And we all do it. We all cut people's throats. Others will always want what you have and you will either kill them to protect it or give it to them out of cowardice."

Sitting there, I remembered my father's unblinking gaze as he watched his friend since childhood burn at the stake. I thought of the strength he must have had not to turn away.

"The truth is, son, everyone makes bargains. They make them with each other. With themselves. With the hard thoughts that creep into their heads at night. They make them with the storms so that they might simply be rain and with each passing winter that it might rest but awhile upon the landscape before quickly moving on again."

"So it's safety, then? Those things protect us?"

"I'm not sure if 'protection' is the word I'd use. A wolf doesn't protect the deer but it does keep the deer in line. Without it, the deer herds would run rampant. They'd overrun what little land they have and eat all the food. Come winter, they'd all be dead from starvation."

"Or someone else would hunt them in the wolves' place."

"You're beginning to understand." My father smiled. A rarity. "The wolf also keeps the deer lean, strong, and alert. Have you heard of this god they have down South? The Christ god? I'm sure you have. Some here claim to follow him but they don't. They can't. The other gods wouldn't allow it."

"I've heard some."

"Well, their god sacrifices himself. Imagine that. Imagine a storm or a wildfire sacrificing itself for a *person*. The idea is ludicrous. They have completely lost touch with the natural order of things. In worshiping a god that dies and resurrects, they have banished the idea of death altogether. The notion has become alien to them. And you know what?"

"What?"

"They have become weak. Soft. Like a deer in a land without wolves. They overrun the continent, mindlessly eating all the food as if it was endless. Mark my words, they'll all be starving soon. Their disconnection with nature will destroy it. Their world will burn because they have forgotten how to live in it. Then do you know what will happen?"

"What will happen?"

"The idea of a god who sacrifices himself will vanish like smoke in the wind. Nature will reestablish itself. And they'll be at each other's throats in no time."

"And our gods," I said. "The ones in the woods. They'll keep them away from us when that happens, right?"

"They will. That's why what Mr. and Mrs. Kristophson did was so short-sighted. In doing what they did, they put the whole town at risk. Not just from outsiders but from the gods themselves. Gods do not like to be tested. One does not trick a blizzard or outwit famine. They do what they will and you just better pray they leave you alone."

I nodded.

My father sighed and I saw the tension go out of his shoulders. He turned and looked at me.

"Someday, you will have children of your own. Even though we're talking about this now, the temptation for wickedness will emerge from the darkest corners of your heart. It will speak falsehoods to you. It will try and convince you to take the easy way out, should the time ever come. But you mustn't. Do you understand?"

"I understand."

"You don't," my father nodded. "But you will."

"How?"

"Time. Time and experience are the only things that

yield true understanding. For now, just know that every time someone draws the red flower, they are partaking in a blessing. They are being invited into the cycle of life and death that acts as the cornerstone of this world. And to spit in its face, as the Kristophsons did, to do that is to spit in the face of the world itself. Remember that when you see the tears and heartbreak."

"And what if I am selected?" I asked. "What if you draw the red flower one day?"

"My heart splits at the thought," my father said honestly. "Half would rest in the blessing, while the other half would wither and harden at the loss of you. But it is those two things come together that make this world worth living. Love for what is and grief for what is lost. They are not opposed to each other but more like opposite feet moving in sequence as you travel through life."

EVEN TO THIS DAY, it is hard for me to parse the truth from my father's words. Sitting here now in the dark and the cold with nothing but ghosts to sorrow my steps, his advice seems like a betrayal. But truth is the truth, despite the path it leads you down.

So as I lay back down in bed and try to quiet the past as it sifts like sand through my head, I try to imagine a different life than this one with different steps and different outcomes. But I know that to do so is nothing but a wish with no one to hear it.

4

They arrive two nights later, just as the sun is setting. I can hear them before I see them. Gunshots, then frantic shouting and jabbering. They must be following the trail, the one that comes from town. The one that leads here.

My rifle is already in my hand when the furious knocking comes. They twist the handle first but it's locked. As they continue to bang on the door, I see a shadow darken the window as someone tries peering in.

"Hello," a voice calls. A man. Young by the sound of it. "Is anyone in there?"

"*Let us in!*" The demand comes right on the heels of the man's plea, but this one is a woman. "Please, there's something out here!"

I close my eyes, rocking back and forth on my feet.

The first thing that comes to mind is the sense of being violated. Who are these people out here on my land disturbing my peace? What do I owe them? Hell, they deserve whatever comes to them, coming out this far. No one comes out here without looking for some sort of *adventure*. Well, they found it.

"*Let us in!*" Another man yells as the door suddenly shakes on its hinges. Or perhaps it's the same man, his voice distorted by anger.

Next, I consider the possibility that this is some sort of trap. I have made it this long by never letting anyone in. Of course, no one other than Alexis has tried but it seems like a solid rule regardless.

Can they do that? Can they warp their voices and appearances? The truth is, I don't know. I know shockingly little about them.

Or maybe these are new creatures. Strangers from a different clan, seeing an open territory with little competition. It's possible. Who knows how many are out there in the dark and forgotten places of the world?

Something suddenly smashes through the glass of the kitchen window. I look over just in time to see an arm jut through. It wraps a curtain in its hand and begins smashing away the jagged pieces of glass still attached to the frame.

Goddamit.

I stomp forward, undo the locks, and throw open the door. Outside stand two women and one man. They look shocked to see me.

"In!" I yell. I turn toward the window, where the head of a large bearded man has appeared. "You too but use the door. Quickly."

They all stumble passed me into the tiny cabin, the bearded guy coming through last. Then, just before I shut the door completely, I spot something standing at the edge of the woods. A little girl in a white snow jacket.

· · ·

AFTER TURNING the lock and throwing the bolts, I turn around and assess the strangers that have just smashed my window and come barging into my home. There are four of them and two of them are holding guns, a dark-haired woman and a bearded man with little pig eyes.

"There's something out there," one of the men croaks. He is clean-shaven with long, brown hair. He is thin, a heavy blaze-orange jacket with bulging pockets dragging him down at the shoulders.

"Were you just going to leave us out there?" Asks one of the women. Her blonde hair is tied back in a ponytail. Blue, spring water eyes wild with indignation.

Beside her, the armed dark-haired woman is quiet, looking almost calm but for an occasional jerky movement as she looks around the cabin. She is short and solidly built, like Tina was.

"Yes," I say, my voice neutral.

The party of four all exchange quick glances.

"What do you mean, *yes*?" Asks the bearded man. The barrel of his weapon begins to drift my way and I return the favor.

"Derek," says the other guy to his friend, a note of urgency in his voice.

"What?" Derek snaps. He swings the shotgun again and I feel the muscles in my stomach clench. "This guy was going to leave us out there for that *thing*."

"What was it that chased you?" I ask, cutting in. I'm not trying to play dumb. I want to know what they know.

"Like a big fucking bat," Derek says. "It gave Katie, *that*." He points at the short dark-haired woman who appears to be bleeding from three deep gouges on her shoulder.

"Did you hit it?"

"What?"

"With your firearms. I heard you shooting."

Derek shakes his head. "I don't know."

"I swear I did," Katie interjects. "I aimed right at it and fired twice. But it didn't go down. It was like I was shooting into nothing."

"What size shot are you using?"

The group is silent for a moment, then the bearded guy tosses me a shell from his vest.

"8-shot," he says and I look down at the brass to see he's correct.

"Birdshot," I say.

They all nod.

"How close were you when you shot it?" I ask the woman named Katie.

She shrugs. "Ten meters maybe. It was hard to tell. It was dark."

"Ten meters is a long way for 8-shot," I say. "You'd be lucky to knock a partridge out of the air from ten meters with this."

"So?" Derek says. "It wasn't like we *weren't* going to shoot. Not after what it did to her."

"I guess what I'm interested in," I say. "Is what you're doing all the way out here in the first place?"

Derek shrugs and makes a face like I'm the dumbest fucking person alive. "*What does it look like*?" He stretches the words out as he says them.

"What I mean is," I let the barrel of my rifle drift quickly across the group and see them all flinch as they look down at it. "What are you doing this far out? What are you doing in my *cabin*?"

"We were on our way to Fort Baron," Sarah says. "It's a five-day trek. There wasn't supposed to be anything here. No roads or trails or towns or nothing. Just raw wilderness. We figured the hunting would be great."

"It's not, by the way," Derek interjects. "We haven't seen anything bigger than a tweety-bird for the last fifteen kilometers."

I don't respond to him. Instead, I think about their story. A five-day trek through the woods. Two of them hunting as they go. Probably fishing. They'd need tents. Sleeping bags. All sorts of stuff.

"Where's your supplies?" I ask.

"Had to drop it," Sarah says. She says it quick enough but not too quick. I believe her.

"No dog?"

They all shake their head.

"Hard to bird hunt without a dog."

"Not if you hit them well enough," Derek says.

He's right. It's a bad attitude to have while hunting but the pig-eyed guy looks dumb enough to believe he can find every bird he wounds on his own and forceful enough to convince everyone else.

So the story isn't made up, I decide. These folks are actually out here on a trip to someplace. But the question is, in all of the hundreds of square kilometers of wilderness, how did they end up at my house?

Then it dawns on me. Something in my face slackens and I sort of slump against the wall behind me. The others notice.

"What?" The long-haired guy asks. "What is it?"

How to say it? How to tell them that the reason they are here right now is because of me? That Alexis *herded* them here like a flock of sheep. She's trying to flush me out. She thinks I'll try and escape with them.

She doesn't know me as well as she thinks she does.

"Nothing," I say, reaching up to rub my forehead. "This is a lot. I don't get many visitors."

"I see that," Sarah says, looking around my cabin.

"Wes," says the long-haired guy after a moment, reaching out his hand.

I look at it for a moment and then shake it hesitantly. "Walter."

An awkward silence passes, then each of the four says their names, one by one. The short, dark-haired woman is Katie, as I had picked up on. The bearded guy is Derek. Blonde Ponytail is Sarah and her husband is Wes.

Four travelers. The first people I have seen other than the bush pilot, Paul Fletcher, since the last of my neighbors walked off into the woods to die. I wonder if these four will share the same fate.

5

———

"So, what are we going to do?" Wes asks. He is sitting in the chair by the window. The one I spend my evening in, talking with Alexis. Sarah has pulled one of the chairs from the kitchen table over to where he is sitting while Derek and Katie are leaning against the wall nearby.

From where I'm sitting on the other side of the room I can tell that Sarah and Wes are in a relationship. Derek and Katie aren't.

"Do you think we could sneak out?" Katie ventures. "Like a backdoor or something? Right before dawn?"

"You'll want to wait until the sun comes up," I say. "She can't go into direct sunlight."

"*She?*" Derek picks up on it. "That thing is a *she*?"

I nod, not feeling like elaborating.

"Okay," Katie continues. "Then we leave at daybreak. As *soon* as the sun is up."

"How far are you away from your vehicles?" I ask.

Silence.

"Two days," Wes finally says. "Probably forty-five hours if we really push it."

I shake my head.

"Really?" Wes asks. "Will it range that far?"

"It's hungry. It's been hungry for some time now."

"What if we kill it?" Derek tries. "We're armed, right? We've got guns."

I feel something inside of me lurch. A protective fear.

"How did that work before?" I ask.

"We'll be closer this time." Derek's face becomes more confident with every word. "We can take it."

"You can't take it. Guns don't work on them."

"*Them?*"

I nod. "There used to be more. They're dead now."

"What happened to them?" Sarah asks. "How'd you kill them?"

"I didn't kill them. They starved. This is the last one."

"You're sure of that?" Wes raises his eyebrows.

"I'm not. But it's the only one I've seen for decades."

"What about wooden stakes?" Katie suggests. "I mean, that's what she is, right? She's a vampire? Shouldn't wooden stakes kill her?"

"I don't know," I admit. "No one has ever gotten close enough to use one. No one has ever tried."

"What about fire? I don't think there's anything living that can-"

"No," I interrupt. "We can't kill her. Better people than you have tried. The only thing I've ever seen work is starvation."

"Could we do that?" Wes asks.

"Starve her? Hell, I'd love to starve her out. I've been trying for decades. Doesn't help that the goddamn meal wagon just rolled in."

"What I mean is, can we wait her out? You must have some contact with the outside world, right?"

"Some," I say, reluctantly.

"Is there a way to contact them?"

"He's a bush pilot. He comes once a year, during the summer."

I let that sink in. The idea of staying cooped up in here for the next nine months or so.

"We can do it," Derek says, a look of resolution on his face. The others seem less certain.

"We don't have enough food," I object. "I barely have enough food for myself. That deer outside should-" My heart skips a beat as I feel the blood drain from my face. I leap out of my chair and run towards the window.

"What?" Wes asks, moving aside.

I don't answer him. Instead, I throw back the curtains to confirm my fear. The deer is gone from the hook. Alexis has taken it.

"Shit," I say.

"What?" Wes repeats.

"The deer I had hanging out there. It's gone."

No one seems to know what that means.

"I had a deer hanging out there," I continue. "It was supposed to feed me for most of the winter."

"Well, you shouldn't have left it *outside*," Derek laughs, his voice edging toward hysteria. "What did you think would happen?"

I don't answer him. I don't tell him that I've left food out there plenty of times before without incident. She's changed something. She's trying to force me out of the cabin. But why now? Is it just the opportunity presented by the hunters?

"Sounds like you're the one being starved out," Sarah

says. If she's trying to keep the cynicism out of her voice, she's doing a bad job.

"We can get food," Wes says.

"How?" Sarah again.

"We'll find a way. We can hunt. Forage. That's what we came out here to do."

"I don't know what you came out here to do," Sarah says. "But I can assure you that *I* didn't come out here to wait in a cabin for nine months while some monster tries to eat us every night."

"We can't be here for *nine months*," Katie adds. "We have lives. Jobs. People who depend on us. We can't just upend all of that."

Something in her face and countenance strikes me just right and in that moment she reminds me of Alexis. She'd be about the same age now.

"I'm not sure we have a choice." Wes's voice is apologetic.

"I still say we try and kill it," Derek says.

"No one's stopping you from trying," Sarah snaps.

Before long, the four of them fall into arguing and I find myself wondering how easy it would be to push all of them back out into the night. I don't want them here. I don't want them sleeping in my house and eating my food.

Something tugs at me though. Something deep down inside of me that can't just throw these folks into the meat grinder out there. I don't know if it's some leftover remnant of human nature or what but it makes me extremely uncomfortable.

What's making me more uncomfortable though is whatever Alexis is doing. Herding these people to my cabin and then stealing my main source of food? She's trying to shake things up. Trying to see if she can take advantage of whatever chaos ensues so she can finally have me.

But why? It should all be the same to her, shouldn't it? Meat is meat. Blood is blood. If she is acting purely out of a need to survive, then why risk the others escaping just so she can have me?

I find myself wondering again how much of Alexis is still in there. I wonder if her memories of me are getting mixed up with her survival instinct, prioritizing me over a sure thing. The truth is, I don't know. I've spent significantly more time with her in her current form now than I ever spent with my daughter. Yet I still know so little about what she's become.

"Everybody stop," Wes yells, silencing the room. "For now, we're going to do our best to hunker down. Once we're good and secure here, we'll try and find a way to kill the thing. But for now, we should get some sleep."

"And what about tomorrow?" Derek asks skeptically.

"Tomorrow, we'll go back and get the packs. It's only a few hours' walk from here, so if we leave early we should be able to get back with plenty of sunlight left. Good?"

No one seems *good* but they accept it at least.

"Good. Now, Walter, do you have any spare blankets or anything?"

"I'll go get the bedrooms ready," I mumble, getting out of the chair. Then, "Don't touch anything."

THE ONLY SPARE bed in the house is in Alexis's room. Some of the parents I knew who had lost their children over the years kept their children's rooms in a state of pure preservation, as if they never left. But only some. Those were the ones who couldn't move on afterwards. And half of them killed themselves before the next winter.

Alexis's room is merely a storage room now. Wooden crates of dried goods and canned vegetables. A few old books. A bed that hasn't been slept in for decades. I walk through to make sure there are no signs of her. I can't have them asking any uncomfortable questions.

Five minutes later, I'm back out with a pile of blankets and two pillows. Wes and Sarah take the room while Derek and Katie set up on opposite sides of the living room. As everyone is getting situated, I survey the place.

Our house was never meant to hold more than three people comfortably and since I lost Tina and Alexis, the building seems to have shrunk in on me. All of the detritus of a solitary life slowly building up like sediment at the mouth of a river.

A gust blows through the room and I realize that the window is still open. I quickly duck back into Alexis's old room, apologize to Wes and Sarah, and sift through some of the junk until I find a couple pieces of sawn lumber and an old blanket. I grab my hammer and a few nails off of one of the shelves in the storage room and then use them to nail the blanket up over the opening, followed by the boards.

When I'm finished, I turn and look at Katie and Derek. I can tell that they're both disturbed by the loud pounding. I get it. They feel vulnerable. They don't want to make any unnecessary noise that might attract any more attention. They don't say anything though, as they're the reason the window is like that in the first place.

I check the locks one more time and feed a few logs into the potbelly stove. I am about to head to bed myself when Katie suddenly asks, "What if we have to go to the bathroom?"

I point at a door with a lantern hanging by it. What I don't do is tell her what it actually is. There is no running water here. No sink and mirror. What I actually have is a long external hallway that branches off of the side of the house and makes an L shape where an enclosed latrine sits.

The place isn't pretty but I've done my best over the years to keep it from being downright horrible. The hole is deep and lined with brick and mortar. The bench with the hole is sanded down. There is a small window above a stone basin with a bucket of fresh water next to it.

Still, there is no soap or toilet paper or whatever else these people might expect. We used to buy those things from Paul when he came through but that was when we had an actual economy in town. When we made things to trade. Now, the only thing I can trade is animal furs and some wood carvings and that barely gets me through the year.

Katie slowly gets to her feet and I turn towards my own door and begin fishing in my pocket for the key. I keep it locked and always will. They don't need to know what's in there.

I manage to get the door open, slip through, and lock it behind me before Katie has time to assess the latrine.

6

I wake up to a quiet knocking. I listen closely for a second, long enough to realize it's not on my own door. For a moment, I think it might be something tapping on my window. Wouldn't be the first time. Thankfully, Alexis realized long ago that I very seldom answer her taps in here. Out in the living room is one thing but it's different to have her coming to me at every hour of the night in the place I feel most secure.

I may have my demons but I have at least established some boundaries.

Getting out of bed, I make my way slowly across the floor. I can tell that the noise is coming from outside my door somewhere off to the right. I'm dressed in my long johns and it takes me a moment to pull my pants and shirt on.

When I step out into the hallway, I see Wes standing at the latrine door. He doesn't acknowledge me, he just knocks a couple more times and says, "*Sarah,*" as quietly as he can.

"What's going on?" I ask, a little annoyed.

"Sarah's been in there a long time," Wes says, still not

looking at me. It's clear he's focused on something. Then I hear it too.

The sound is something between a whisper and a rasp, like two pieces of paper sliding over each other. But as I listen to it more, focusing in, it begins to sound wetter. A rhythmic pulse.

"What's going on?" Katie joins us at the door, looking how I feel. A mix of curiosity and annoyance.

I don't answer her question though. Instead, I pull on the door handle. For as long as the house has been standing, there has been a small piece of wood on the inside of the latrine door that lowers down into an open latch and serves as a sort of lock. I haven't used it for years but I can tell it's in place now.

Thankfully, it's not too strong.

"Wait, what are you-" Wes says as I suddenly throw my weight against the door.

The wooden latch holds but I feel it bend. I hit it again and this time there is the sound of a million tiny splinters as it begins to break. I step back and aim a foot squarely at the handle and kick as hard as I can.

There is a loud crash as the door slams inward and bangs off of the back wall. I'm inside in an instant, Wes and Katie right behind me. The light is low, the lit lantern out of view on the bench. It casts a golden hue on a sight that makes my blood run cold.

Sarah is pressed up against the tiny window, her body undulating slightly. Pieces of broken glass glint dully on the floor. Once again, it sounds like she's whispering. But as we get closer I realize it's more of a sucking, gulping sound.

I place my hand on her shoulder to turn her around and as I do her head wobbles and then falls backward at an impossible angle. Her throat has been ripped through right to the spine and the ragged flesh stares up at me like a gory maw.

"*No!*" Wes howls as he tries to rush forward. I block his way though. Or, more accurately, I am frozen in place.

The sight that has me planted to the spot is not the ravaged neck of Sarah's lifeless corpse but the face staring at me through the shattered window.

Alexis has her mouth wide open in a savage smile twice as wide as any normal human mouth can go. Her jaw is hanging crooked to one side, endless rows of translucent teeth jutting out. Her eyes are wild, her pupils dilated. I stand transfixed for a singular moment as I stare at the morbid parody of what was once my daughter.

Then her lower jaw makes a loud clacking sound as it slides back into place. And in the next moment, she is swallowed by the night outside.

"How could this happen?" Wes is distraught. He's been pacing for the last five minutes, not letting anyone get a word in edgewise. "You said that thing couldn't get in here if it wasn't invited."

"It *didn't* get in," I say, waiting for him to cut me off again. When he doesn't, I continue. "I've suspected for some time that she has some sort of hypnotic power. My guess is, she lured Sarah to the window and convinced her to break the glass."

"She wouldn't do that," Wes says. His voice is raspy from sobbing earlier. He's cried out for now and that inexplicable grief seems to have transformed into rage. "She's not that stupid."

"It's not about being smart or stupid. It's about willpower."

"Then why the fuck didn't you warn us?" He shouts.

"I assumed you would all use caution. And like I said, I didn't know for sure. I still don't. None of us were there."

Wes is shaking his head. I see him glance towards the shotguns that are laid out on the kitchen table and I don't know if he's thinking about shooting the vampire or shooting me.

"Anything else you haven't told us?" Derek pipes up.

"There's a lot I haven't told you. Truth is, I wouldn't have the time to tell it if you stayed here five years."

"He keeps his door locked." Katie's voice is small. "I saw it on the way to the bathroom. He keeps it locked."

Everyone turns to look at me.

"Would you keep your door locked if you lived here alone with that thing outside?"

"What are you keeping in there," Derek asks, ignoring my challenge.

"None of your business."

"I think we have a right to know," he says. "I think that we-"

"This is my house," I yell. "*My. House.* I could be keeping a dancing goose that lays golden eggs and burps the alphabet in there and it wouldn't be any of your goddamn business. You are not *welcome* here. I do not *want* you here. The only reason that I haven't booted your asses out the door yet is because I don't want to make her any stronger than she already is."

Everyone is quiet.

"Now, I'm going to go back to bed," I continue. "Because I assume that tomorrow is going to be another long and terrible day. I'm going to lock the door behind me and if anyone tries to get in, I'm going to put a .308 slug right through the middle of it. So everyone shut the fuck up. Mind your own business. And go back to sleep."

The room looks shocked, all of the previous day's struggles and anxieties suddenly plain on their faces. They're scared. They're grieving. And they just got yelled at by the raging madman they have chosen to lock themselves inside with.

And I couldn't care less.

DESPITE MY DECLARATION of needing sleep, I lay awake staring at the ceiling.

I can't think about the strangers in my living room. Can't think about the dead woman's head falling back to reveal her ruined neck. Of my daughter's gleeful face smeared with blood staring at me through broken glass.

Instead, I think of a memory I've come back to time and time again over the years. I haven't really figured it out, to be honest. Not that it needs figuring out. It's just some instance that happened to leave a troublesome indent on me.

We were out on Big Harriet Lake in April. There was still ice on the lake thick enough to walk on. We didn't venture too far out. Maybe twenty meters where the water below would barely reach your waist if you were to step down into it. Any further out and we would have encountered big patches of open water where the lake was fed by underground springs.

The sky was naked blue over us. Tina had broken a hole through the ice and was dangling a line in the water. Every couple of seconds, she would twitch her finger, jigging the piece of bread she had attached to the hook across the bottom of the lake. A pile of bled fish lay in the snow next to her, their eyes staring wide at nothing.

The blood made me nauseous, I remember, the small cuts that Tina made behind the sunfish's gills still oozing. I've had to kill a lot of animals in my life and have encountered more than my fair share of blood. Even so, I was never comfortable with it. Hot and sticky, boiling as it splashed down onto my face from Mrs. Kristophson's ruined corpse.

Alexis was with us. She was maybe three years old at the time. Four months before her mother's suicide. About a year and a half from when I lifted the jar and revealed the red flower.

By this point, she knew well enough to stay away from the open water. She had taken a spill in one of her mother's fishing holes a month back. She didn't go all the way in and we were right there to quickly haul her out but the incident made an impression on her.

Now, she kept pretty close to us out there and made sure to watch her step and steer clear of any open water.

That day, she had taken to making snowballs. The weather was beginning to warm up and the snow was nice and packy. She made ball after ball, stacking them in a neat little pyramid. Once she finished with one pyramid she would begin the next.

She was on her fourth little snowball pyramid when there was a deep groan beneath us. There was a sound like that of bending sheet metal, a sound I had heard thousands of times before. The ice was shifting.

A deafening crack split the air as the ice beneath Alexis's feet began to rock and then a sheet of it broke off with her on it and began drifting out into the open water. She seemed shocked at first, frozen where she stood. Then she tried to walk towards the edge, causing the sheet to tilt slightly. Taking a few quick steps back, she righted the balance and stared at us hopelessly.

I ran to the edge of the ice and stared across the lengthening gap of water, my heart hammering in my chest. Before I knew what I was doing, I was stripping off my jacket, snow pants, and boots.

"I'll get a rope," Tina yelled as she bolted in the opposite direction.

I braced myself, trying not to think about how cold the water would be. Cold did not describe it. Diving headfirst, the frigid water hit me like a closed fist. The adrenaline pumping through me dulled the sensation, however, and I burst through the surface.

It only took a few seconds for me to reach the sheet that Alexis was on but once I did, I struggled with the best way to get her off of it. If I plunged her into the water with me, she had a much greater chance of freezing to death due to her tiny body. I tried gripping the ice and pulling it back but to no avail. It was too large.

My clothes felt heavy around me and the numbing sensation that had begun to penetrate every inch of my body told me that I only had a short amount of time to accomplish this. Eventually, I decided to risk it.

"Come to me, sweetie," I said, gesturing for Alexis to join me.

She edged backwards a bit further, her eyes wide with fear. Her arms were clutched tightly around herself. She shook her head.

"It's okay, I got you." I couldn't feel my feet anymore. I was still treading water but I didn't think I'd be able to walk if I tried.

She still didn't come forward.

"Hey sweetie," I looked into her eyes, pouring as much

comfort into her as I could across that bare and lonely distance. "I won't let anything happen to you."

In that moment, I believed it with all of my heart. I would have sacrificed my own life for her in an instant. My face must have conveyed it because she finally began inching forward.

With our combined weight on the ice, the sheet tilted more this time. Alexis took a few more steps and then she was falling down into my arms as the sheet finally tipped her off her feet. Her body hit me more forcefully than I expected and pushed my head beneath the water for a few seconds. I soon managed to regain my equilibrium though and began kicking even harder.

Using my arm to paddle in a half circle, I got turned around and began making my way slowly back to where Tina was waiting with the rope. Alexis got situated on my shoulders so only her legs got wet and once I made it to Tina I was able to spill her off onto the ice, where she immediately scrambled away from the edge.

By this time, my fingers were completely numb and I had to wrap my arm around the rope so Tina could haul me up onto the ice. Once out of the water, I lay there wracked with violent shivers as Tina rushed Alexis inside to sit by the fire. Three minutes later and I was inside as well.

Neither of us suffered any serious damage. The water had been freezing but we were inside fast enough to prevent any long-term effects. But I find myself thinking about that day a lot. I thought of it often immediately afterward and I thought of it on my walk back from the clearing after leaving Alexis there.

The look of uncertainty in her eyes as the ice drifted slowly away from us. The change in her expression when she chose to trust me and jump onto my shoulders. All of that swirls around with the screams of the children that were ripped from their family's arms as punishment for the Kristophson's betrayal. The hard but wise words from my father as he sat with me.

The sum of all of those moments has left me with a sense of pain and indecision that is borderline unfathomable. And if the tableau of all of those memories has a face, it isn't the indecision on Alexis's face that day as she found herself stranded on the ice. And it isn't the searing pain of Mrs. Kristophon's blood scarring me for life.

If anything, the face of all these moments was a face I saw tonight. My daughter, dead and smiling, wearing another woman's blood across her cheeks and lips. Jagged teeth and feral eyes, slithering back into the inky darkness beyond the light.

7

The light of the next morning is a hazy grey that filters into my room through the cracks in the curtains. The prospect of having to hike out with at least one of the hikers hangs over me like an ax and it briefly occurs to me that it might not be a bad place to ditch one of these intruders for good.

I immediately wipe the thought from my mind though as I get dressed. After all those years of being complicit in the sacrifice of children followed by many more years of isolation, it's difficult not to see this as a chance to reassert myself as part of humankind. Not as someone who trades their neighbor's lives for safety but as someone who stands with them against the odds.

Just another complicating factor roiling around in my thoughts this morning.

In the living room, everyone is already up and awake. Derek and Katie look like shit. Wes looks like whatever shit shits. It's obvious that no one got very much sleep the previous night.

We make a light breakfast of jam and birds' eggs. As I'm

cracking one of the eggs open however, I notice that there is a tiny bird embryo inside of one of them. It's thin and naked, its eyes closed. I shake it lightly and it doesn't move.

I stare at it for a beat longer than I should. The image of its curled little frame that will never wake stirring something. This isn't the first egg I've found like this. It's often times difficult to see how far along they are when you take them from the nest. But this time is different.

Or maybe the circumstances are different. A lot has been dredged up over the last day and I feel the urge to cradle the tiny body in the palm of my hand. To carry it as a memento of things lost.

I chuck it in the bin in the corner and cover it with the various items of refuse around it.

"Weather doesn't look great," I say.

"Think it'll rain?" Wes asks from beside me as we make our way down the overgrown path.

"Possibly."

We've been hiking for about an hour. Wes and I are out in front while Derek and Katie bring up the rear. The trail is narrow and brush encroaches from both sides, occasionally forcing us into a single-file line.

"How safe are we if a bunch of dark storm clouds roll in?" Wes's countenance is better than what I expected, considering he lost his wife the night before. I've seen survival do that to people though. Life and death circumstances have a way of bringing the strength out of some folks.

"Depends on how dark they are," I say. "She should be sleeping right now but if a big storm wakes her up then we might be in trouble."

"We should pick up the pace then."

THE PACKS ARE FARTHER AWAY than I expected and it's late morning by the time we reach them.

"You ran all this way?" I ask.

"We did," Katie says, breathing hard.

"It seems like a lot further of a distance when you're walking it in the daytime," Wes adds. "But when we were running last night, it was like time and fatigue ceased to exist. There was only escape."

"Speak for yourself," Derek says, breathing hard. "I thought I was going to collapse. It felt like we ran *forever*."

Just then, a roll of distant thunder echoes off in the distance. We all turn and look. The packs were dropped right there on the trail with tall stands of trees rising up in all directions so it is difficult to see how big the oncoming storm is. Still, I feel warning bells begin to ring inside of me.

"We should get moving," I say.

WE'RE ABOUT HALFWAY BACK when it begins to rain. It starts with a few drops and then gradually increases in strength.

"Big rain, little rain. Little rain, big rain," Katie shouts from behind us.

"What?" I turn around but keep moving forward.

"It's something my dad says. Apparently, if rain comes on really hard then it's probably not going to last for very long. But if it starts small and grows, then you're in for a big storm."

I think of all of the storms I've ever experienced to try and decide if what she's saying is true. I can think of some exceptions like light rain showers in the spring and heavy downpours that seemed like they lasted for days. But overall, I can't really tell one way or the other if what she's saying rings true.

One thing that is true, however, is that the sky is growing noticeably darker. I lean forward and pick up the pace even more.

WE'RE RUNNING by the time the first crack of lightning illuminates the sky. There are a few times when the path ahead seems to disappear in the low light, leaving nothing but a wall of trees. When this happens, I usually have to slow down and try and discern the way.

One advantage to the trail, however, is that the shrubs and long grass offer signs of our passing earlier that day. Bent stalks and broken twigs. Enough for a tracker to follow but not particularly quickly. It's enough though when we find ourselves suddenly uncertain of the path ahead.

Another good thing is that all of the brush in the trail keeps the dirt firm. No loose mud from the rain or washed-out areas. The roots of the vegetation keep the ground stable beneath us as we plod our way forward.

I imagine the four of them dashing through the woods the previous night as the sun set around them. It wasn't raining then but the path would have still been difficult to navigate. The more I think about it, the more clear it is that they were being herded by Alexis. Pushing them in the direction she wanted them to go. Pushing them towards me.

The packs are heavy on our backs, the straps digging into our shoulders as they bounce.

"Are these waterproof?" I yell behind me to Wes.

"What?" The sound of the rain nearly drowns out his voice.

"The packs," I yell. "Are they waterproof?"

"Yes," he yells back. "Why?"

"I think we should ditch them."

"We're so close though. And I don't know how well they'd do just laying out here. Plus, I think the chances are good she'll take them. Like she took the deer."

That didn't occurred to me but he's right. If we ditch the packs now then we'll probably never see them again. The chances of there being enough food in them to make much of a difference is low but I've had some lean winters. Winters where each individual can of vegetables felt like a blessing. Every piece of leathery dried meat: a revelation. I know that ultimately, a little food can go a long way.

But I also know that it won't matter if everyone's dead.

I want to continue the conversation but yelling back and forth as we run through a sopping wet forest with thirty-kilogram packs on our backs has taken a lot out of me. Plus, the woods are looking more and more familiar. We're close.

Someone from behind yells something but I can't make it out. I turn quickly to see if I can get a glimpse of the hikers but this part of the trail is dense and all I see is the tangle of wet branches. I power forward, hoping they follow me.

The trail ahead begins to open up. If it was a clear night then we would probably be able to see the lights from my house through the branches by now. I hit something of a straightaway and halfway down it, I look back.

Everyone is still coming. I can see Wes followed by Katie and I assume Derek is close behind. Katie's face is pale though and Wes looks frantic.

"What is it?" I slow down a bit.

"We saw something," Katie says. "I think it was her."

"She looked normal." Wes is shaking his head. "Like a little girl. Derek tried going towards her at first but she was in a pretty dark part of the woods. Off the trail. He said something felt wrong so he backed off."

"Did you see her?"

"Yes," he puffs. He's visibly out of breath. "Katie and I both saw her just now. Same situation. She just stood there under a tall pine tree, smiling."

I look back and see that Derek has just come into view. He's moving about as fast as his exhausted body will allow him.

"Walter...She looked like the girl last night. The one that-" He can't finish the sentence.

"Whatever you do," I yell, making sure everyone can hear me. "Don't approach the girl."

I expect a smart-ass remark but all I get are nods. Everyone just wants to get back to the house.

Suddenly, I see Wes's face go white. He's looking at something over my shoulder. He slows his pace and I turn to see what he's looking at.

And there she is, standing barely an arm's length from me. The sight of her takes my breath away. I stumble to a halt.

She's standing in a thicket of pines, a couple of tall aspens giving her just enough cover. If it was a normal day with a clear blue sky, she'd have no chance. But even in the last five minutes, the world seems to have grown darker. Thunder booms across the sky as the rain continues its onslaught.

Alexis wears a shy smile, water dripping from her wet hair. She looks up at the dark clouds above and slowly extends her hand out of the shadows. Thin wisps of pale blue smoke emerge from her bare fingers.

I want to take her hand. I want to pull her out of the

dark, out of the past, out of this nightmare. I want to pull her to me and hold her tight, damn the consequences.

"Hi, papa."

The sound of her voice breaks the illusion. So many nights of hearing it through the glass of my living room window. So many nights of torturing myself. What I just now realize is that all of those nights have had the effect of desensitizing me to the charade. By this point, I have had five times the amount of conversations with the dead Alexis than the real one. My experience of her is now predominantly one of subterfuge and when she speaks, I am reminded of that fact.

Sorrow floods my heart. Sorrow at the slow diminishing of the fantasy over the years. That poisonous refuge I have abided in for so long, finally showing the cracks in the framework. Sorrow at the damage it's done to the real memories of my daughter. The tainting of the only real thing I have left of her.

I turn and bolt, the others close behind me. The house is near. I know exactly where we are now. Just around the next corner and-

An audible snap comes from behind me, followed by the unmistakable sound of someone's body collapsing to the ground. I turn just in time to see Wes cry out in pain. Katie skids to a halt while Derek muscles his way past her.

"C'mon! Derek yells as he runs. In no time, he has made his way past Katie and Wes and is out in front of us. He slows briefly and repeats himself. "*C'mon.*"

He keeps glancing over at the thicket Alexis was in and then scanning the skyline. I turn back around and see that Alexis is gone.

Moving quickly, I dash over to help Katie as she slowly drags Wes to his feet. It's then that I see the large and slippery rock behind him. He's favoring his left leg as he gets upright.

"My ankle," he gasps. "It's-"

"Worry about it later," I snap. "We have to move."

With Katie on his left side and me on his right, we stumble out into the clearing and see the house. Derek has the door open and is beckoning us to hurry. Then, his expression changes as he sees something behind us. He disappears into the house.

The sky is black now. So black it might as well be night. Katie and I are sprinting, Wes's good foot skipping occasionally. I find myself wishing I could ditch the packs but they're on too tight. It would take too much time to shrug them off. Time we can't afford.

Derek reappears in the doorway with one of the shotguns. He's still loading shells into the tube when I'm hit from the side.

The world tumbles around me as all three of us are sent sprawling. Arms and legs grasping and kicking in every direction as we scramble on the ground. There's a loud *boom* followed by two more in quick succession.

Staggering back to my feet, I see Derek firing the shotgun. He pulls the trigger and the muzzle flashes like lightning in the dark of the storm. He pumps an empty shell out onto the ground and fires again. Then nothing. He scrambles in his pockets for more ammunition.

Katie and I are back up, followed quickly by Wes. This time I feel it coming. A gust of foul air. The dull beat of leathery wings. I duck just in time to see Katie and Wes get knocked off their feet by a dark shape.

She's playing with us. I don't know why but she is.

Then it dawns on me. I look at the two on the ground, dazed and trying to rise for a second time. I think of Wes and his broken ankle. I think of the winter to come. I make my choice.

"What are you doing?" Katie screams as I drag her to the door. I see her look behind me at Wes. "*Stop!*"

Then we're at the door. I let go of Katie and Derek grabs ahold of her. She tries breaking free of his grip but he's too strong. He drags her inside.

Only when I'm within the threshold of the house do I finally turn to see Wes. He's about four meters away, swaying on his one good leg. I look into his eyes and acceptance dawns on his face.

Alexis hits him from behind like an eagle, her talons digging into his shoulders. He cries out as he is lifted into the air. Four bat-like limbs scrabble at his body in a way that reminds me of a spider attacking some helpless insect. Wes is turned upright and then Alexis begins tearing at his throat. He screams, the screams quickly turning into a sort of howling garble.

Katie wails from behind me as she watches the horrible display, then I find myself shoved aside as Derek pushes past with the shotgun. He puts the weapon to his shoulder and fires three times, Wes's blood-soaked shirt plucking up in multiple places with each deafening boom.

Alexis seems utterly unaffected by it. She has her mouth pressed hard into Wes's savaged neck now and I can see her entire body pulse as she drains him. The whole process is over in seconds.

Once she is finished, Alexis looks down at the three of us. That same horrid face. Half-human, half-demon. She stares for a few moments, then with a deft movement of her powerful hands, she tears Wes's head from his body, the whole spinal column coming with it.

Katie sobs behind me, the guttural sounds of her crying

punctuated by the metallic click of Derek loading more shells into the shotgun. It seems that Alexis isn't keen to be shot at anymore, because before Derek can put the weapon to his shoulder again, she lobs Wes's head down at us and then flies off into the storm.

The head lands just beyond the step, bouncing and rolling to a stop in front of us. The expression on his face is oddly peaceful. His eyes are closed, mouth slightly open. He could just as well be sleeping.

8

The rain pounds on the roof for another few hours as the storm rages. We remove our packs and place them in the center of the small living room before changing out of our wet clothes. A long time passes before anyone says anything.

Once the sounds of thunder fade off into the distance and the rain dies down to a steady tapping, Katie finally speaks up.

"You left him."

I don't respond. I don't justify it. I think she's going to repeat the words again but she doesn't. Instead, the three of us just sit there silently in the truth of what just happened.

"We should take stock of what's in the packs," Derek finally says. The man is more deflated than I've seen him and it suddenly occurs to me that Katie could just as well have been talking to him. After all, he didn't make any move to help Wes after he fell on the trail.

We set about removing everything from the wet packs and dividing it into piles. They begin with clothes first. Katie puts her clothes off to the side and then begins sorting through Wes's stuff as his shirts and jeans are a better fit for her than Sarah's. She takes Sarah's undergarments though and puts them with her stuff. At first, I think it's out of some sense of modesty for the woman, like she doesn't want a man touching them, but then I see that they are made out of some kind of stretchy material that will likely fit Katie as well.

After the clothes, we make a pile for tools. There are a few sets of pliers, two hatchets, ten boxes of waterproof matches, three knives of varying length, a few spools of thin rope, and a few other trinkets that I couldn't quite discern a use for.

Finally, we get to the food, which ends up being more than I thought. Between dried fruit, dried meat, some assorted nuts, and a bunch of brightly packaged treats that I have never seen before there is probably enough to last us a month if we portion it out extremely conservatively. There is also a healthy assortment of tin plates, cups, and silverware.

Aside from the different piles of stuff, there are a few odd pieces like a small tackle box and retractable fishing rod, gun-cleaning kit, rolled up gun cases, three collapsable tents, four sleeping bags and pillows, one large pot, two pans, some towels of varying sizes, and one liter of blended whiskey.

It's been a long time since I've had a drink of alcohol. Between the depression and increased possibility of making some mistake that might get me killed, I simply couldn't afford it. Still, the golden brown liquor practically calls to me from the glass bottle. One whole liter of forgetting. Liquid oblivion, poured neat.

The hikers have packed in a lot of stuff, considering. No wonder the packs were so heavy.

The most important thing is obviously the food.

Everything else, excluding the brightly colored treats and stretchy underwear, is stuff that I have access to in my home or in the abandoned buildings in town.

"You should decide who gets the bed," I say as we finish organizing the stuff.

There is a brief pause as Katie and Derek look at each other, then Katie looks back at me and says, "I don't think either of us feel like sleeping in there right now, thanks."

From the look on Derek's face, it's clear that he doesn't feel the same way but he keeps quiet. Katie is obviously still torn up about Wes and Sarah. But still, I push a little more.

"You'll sleep better in there. You can take turns if you-"

"No one is going to be sleeping well for a *while*," Katie snaps, her face flush.

"Derek," I say. "How about you take the room first."

Neither of them respond. I leave the room. There's still a lot of work to be done but I'm all but drowning in these people's emotions right now. It's more than I've experienced in a long time and I've forgotten how exhausting the whole routine is.

When I come back out in a few hours, I see that Derek has set up in the spare bedroom.

I MAKE a big meal that night. Venison backstraps cooked in rendered beaver fat. Mushrooms and wild onions. Pickled carrots and cucumbers.

I'm not sure what has inspired me to do so. Maybe it's because I had such a small breakfast and no lunch. Maybe my body is crying out for nutrients after the dash through the woods today. Or maybe I simply wanted to impress these people. To break bread with them. The first taste of community I've experienced in ages.

Maybe it's not nutrients I'm starved for.

Regardless of how I'm feeling, neither of my two guests seem particularly hungry. They still eat, Derek more than Katie, but they hardly pack it in like I'd expect a couple people who've just survived insurmountable odds and been in the bush for the last three days would.

Maybe I've become immune to tragedy. Maybe this is what normal people are like after seeing someone torn apart in front of their eyes.

Without thinking, I reach up and touch the burn mark on the left side of my face.

"How do you all know each other?" I ask, the question directed at both of them.

They seem shocked by it, their mouths chewing a little slower than they were a second ago. Derek is the one who finally speaks.

"Wes was my college roommate." He points at Katie. "Katie was childhood friends with Sarah. Wes and Sarah met at a wedding about a year after we graduated and the rest is history."

"You two know each other through Wes and Sarah."

They both nod. The conversation is awkward but I try to push through it.

"What's college?"

"Hmm?" Derek gives me a funny look.

"College. You said you met Wes there."

He blinks a few times, then says, "It's like a school. Do you have a school here?"

"No, but I've heard of schools. We mostly teach our own children here."

Derek shakes his head. "Man, what is this place? How is it possible this place has existed for so long without anyone finding out about it?"

"We were protected," I say before I can stop myself.

"Protected?" Katie speaks up. "What the fuck does that mean?"

My mind races as I try to figure out an adequate lie. Instead, I end up settling on the truth, though a sanitized version of it.

"That thing out there. There used to be more of them." I feel my eyes bounce back and forth between the two of them. "We weren't always...enemies..."

Both of their eyebrows lift practically off of their faces.

"What do you mean *not enemies*?" Derek says, incredulous. "What, were they like, your *dogs* or something?"

"More like, we were theirs. They protected us from the outside world. From the chaos of the cities and your god who kills himself."

"Our...*what*?"

"My father and mother-in-law told me about your god. How he does not require sacrifice. How *he* is the sacrifice."

"I think he means Jesus," Katie says, half-turning to Derek. Then, "Look, there are a *lot* of different people with a *lot* of different religions where we're from. I don't think either Derek or I are Christians. In fact, we're not even religious. I consider myself a *spiritual* person but that's about it."

"I was raised Catholic if that means anything," Derek says.

I shake my head, uncomprehending. "You have no gods?"

"Not really, no," Katie says.

"Then who do you sacrifice to?"

An uncomfortable look passes between them, then Katie says, "No one. No one sacrifices anything."

"How can that be? How can you live your life without sacrifice?"

"I mean, we sacrifice our time and money but not like...*animals*."

"Who do you sacrifice your time and money to?"

Katie shrugs. "I don't know, ourselves. Our families."

"I don't understand."

"And I don't understand what *you don't* understand." Katie seems genuine.

"Walter," Derek says slowly. "What do *you* sacrifice to?"

The question hits me like a slap. This conversation has not in any way gone like I was hoping. Finally, I say, "No one, I guess. Not for a long time. But it's just me out here. No family. No community. You have to understand, I do my best to survive out here but I don't-" A sigh escapes my lips. "-I don't really care about protection or anything. I don't care if I live, ultimately."

Silence settles like a stone at the bottom of a lake. Katie shifts uncomfortably as Derek fiddles with his fingers.

"You say it's just you out here," Katie says. "Did you used to have someone? A family, I mean?"

I see the question coming from a long ways off. I'm prepared for it.

"I did," I say hesitantly. "A wife and daughter. Then those things came. Or rather, they turned on us."

"What changed?"

"I've been asking myself that for a long time. Best I can figure, food got scarce. Deer, bears, wolves, bobcats, squirrels. They all disappeared. Then there was nothing left but us."

"That thing we saw in the woods today," Derek says. "It looked human. *Was* it human?"

"No," I lie.

"Really, because I've heard my fair share of vampire stories and-"

"You've heard wrong," I snap. "This isn't a story. She isn't —that isn't a person. She's a monster. A monster that likes to play tricks. Simple as that."

MY SLEEP IS restless tonight as images reel endlessly through my head. Alexis's blood-smeared face. Wes's head being torn off and thrown to the ground. A baby bird, dead in its shell. Children burning. Flapping leathery wings. My father's smiling face, warm and gentle. Tina with a rope around her neck, her tongue inflated and purple. Fish bleeding into the snow.

Alexis on a sheet of ice, drifting away.

I awake to the sound of pounding again. But this time, it's not the latrine door. It's mine.

"Hold on," I yell as I pull on my pants and over-shirt. The banging continues.

When I finally open the door to yell my obscenities at whoever's knocking, the words never make it out. Instead, the wooden stock of a shotgun crashes into my face.

9

———

The taste of blood fills my mouth as I stumble backwards, falling against the foot of the bed and slipping down to the floor.

"What the fuck are you doing?" I yell through my bloody teeth.

"*No,*" Derek yells, "What the fuck are-"

The second half of the sentence dies in his throat as he sees what I have piled floor-to-ceiling in my room. Katie runs in and sees me on the ground, then does a double take at what Derek is looking at.

"Walter," she says slowly. "What is this?"

I glance over at the other half of the room where I have roughly forty-five tanks of propane, each the size of my chest, stacked on top of each other.

"I keep it in here so she doesn't take it," I say.

"But you have nothing that hooks up to propane," Derek says. "You're using oil lanterns and a wood stove that you cook on. What could you possibly need this much for?"

He's got the shotgun down at his hip, aimed generally in my direction. The birdshot he has in there wasn't near enough to put a scratch on Alexis but at this range, it stands a good chance of being lethal.

"Other houses have propane stoves and heating," I say. "Sometimes in the winter-"

"Hey Walter," Derek says softly. "How about you stop fucking lying."

I don't say anything.

"I know you've been lying since we got here. About that thing outside. About your creepy little town. About everything."

"Derek," Katie tries. "Maybe we should calm down."

"No, I'm done being calm. We've been listening to him for the last twenty-four hours and in that time, Wes and Sarah have died. So yeah, I'm done being calm and I'm done listening to him tiptoe around what's really going on here."

"What do you think is going on here?" I ask, shaking my head slowly.

Derek reaches into his back pocket and pulls something out. It looks like a small picture frame. He shows it to Katie and I see her expression change. First, incomprehension. Then confusion. Then, anger. She turns towards me as Derek throws the picture down at my feet.

I don't need to look at it. I already know what it is.

"Where'd you find it?" I ask.

"At the back of the dresser in the room, behind a bunch of clothes."

"You were going through my stuff?"

"Yes." His voice is ice-cold. "I was."

I reach down and pick up the picture frame, then climb slowly to my feet, making sure I don't startle him and end up with a fistful of lead in my stomach. The picture is one of the few I have of Alexis. A Polaroid that one of the neighbors down the street took for us.

Alexis in a blue cotton dress with white shoes. A warm, summer day. Green maple trees in the background. A sliver of bright blue sky at the edge of the frame. I stuffed the picture in a drawer not long after leaving her in the clearing that day. It was too much. Too real. I found that I much preferred my fantasy version.

"My daughter," I say, letting the tiredness leak into my voice. "Her name is Alexis."

"She's the girl we saw in the woods," Derek says. "The thing that's been hunting us. Killing us. You lied when you said she was never a human. She's your own damn daughter."

"I don't see how it matters."

"I just spent the last hour alone in that room thinking the same thing. How does this matter? How does this change things? And most importantly, why would you lie about it?"

"My mother always told me that some wounds are best left beneath a bandage. I just wanted some privacy."

"That's the obvious answer, right?" Derek shrugged. "Poor Walter is so broken up about his dead little girl that he doesn't feel comfortable talking about it. So instead he lies. But then another question began tickling the back of my mind. Can you guess what it is?"

I don't say anything. Instead, it's Katie who speaks up.

"Why are we here?"

"Bingo," Derek says.

"I don't understand."

"Yes you do, Walter."

And the truth is, I do. I just hoped that they didn't.

"This whole time we've been here," Katie says. "I've been thinking the same thing: how lucky we were to stumble upon one of the only living people for hundreds of square kilometers. But it wasn't luck, was it?"

"No," Derek says before I can answer. "That thing led us here. Pushed us here. Herded us inside your shitty little house like pigs to the slaughter. Watching her today, it occurred to me that she could have killed all four of us before we even had our packs off. Yet, she chose to pick at us and harry us down the trail right to your place."

"So," I say.

"So, she doesn't want us. She wants *you*."

"We're a bunch of unknown variables," Katie says. "My guess is that she's been trying to snag you for a very long time. And now she sees this as her chance."

"Why would she do that?" I argue. "She's just an animal now. A hungry one. Meat is meat."

"Maybe she figured she had a better chance of getting you with us in the house," Derek theorizes. "She's been trying to get you for years. Maybe even decades. Maybe she thought she could throw a wrench into your normal routine, causing you to slip up somewhere. Then she just picks *us* off at her leisure. She's already proven pretty capable of that."

"Or," Katie says. "Maybe she just wants you because you're her father. Maybe it's personal. I don't understand how the mind of that creature works but who knows? Maybe there's still some part of her that wants her daddy. Even if the only way she can have him is torn and bleeding in her claws."

It surprises me how cold Katie's voice is. I can tell that, in this moment, she hates me. She hates me for all of the grief I've caused her. They both do.

Derek walks slowly over to the pile of propane tanks while I back into the corner. Katie watches me but doesn't stop me. She sees me moving toward the window and I can see the wheels turning in her head. The scene playing out.

She's imagining me hurling myself through the glass out into the night. She and Derek rush over to see me make it a few yards before I'm ripped off my feet into the air by the thing that killed their friends.

I see her thinking it. I see her craving it.

"You know what I think?" Derek says.

I don't answer him.

"I think the reason you have these propane tanks in here is because one day, maybe not too long from now, you plan on blowing yourself up. Maybe you tell yourself that it's for your daughter. That you'll find some way to trap her somewhere and send her ass sky high in a ball of fire." He puts his hands on one of the dark green tanks. "But deep down, you know they're for you. I don't know what went down with your family but I bet you feel really guilty about it whatever it was."

I remain silent, moving closer to the window with each passing breath.

"You asked us this evening about sacrifice," Derek says. "And when I asked you about it you neatly side-stepped the question. But I think I have the answer. I think your god is your conscience. You've been denying that god your whole life but when you finally reach the end, you're going to pay him back in one big spectacular ball of flame. You might not know it yet but that's exactly what you're planning."

"Maybe," I croak out. "Would you like to know what *I* think?"

Derek turns to face me. Sees that I'm right in front of the window now. He doesn't make any move towards me.

"I think you're scared," I say. "I think you're scared to be out here because you're afraid of what a few months in this place will do to you. You're afraid you'll become like me." I turn to Katie.

"I've seen children die," I say. "I've watched them torn from their mother's arms and tied to a stake and burned alive, only to be ripped away by monsters at the last second. I found my wife hanging in the storage room because she couldn't live with what this life demanded of her. And it wasn't until after I walked my own daughter out into a clearing to be eaten that I realized she made the right choice."

Something twists in Katie's face. Some potent mix of sadness and revulsion.

"But when I saw you firing that shotgun at my daughter today, Derek, I realized something too. I realized that, even though she's a monster, I still love her. I still fear for her. And I'm sorry."

"Sorry for what?" Derek snaps.

"I'm sorry that your friends died. I'm sorry for lying to you. And most of all, I'm sorry for what comes next."

"Me too," Derek says, the barrel of the shotgun begins to swing toward me.

I can see his heart isn't in it. He wants me dead but he doesn't want to do it himself. He wants me to jump through the window that I've positioned myself in front of. To die the same way his friends died.

Unfortunately for him, I'm not going to do that. I have a daughter to take care of and the window isn't the only thing over here. With the determination of a father who finally knows what it means to protect his family, I reach quickly beneath the pillow in front of me.

Derek freezes. The gun trembles, then goes off. A few of the tiny pieces of shot hit me in the left arm, stinging like bees while the rest of the load tears apart the wall behind me. For all intents and purposes, he's missed. I don't.

The revolver is up before he can jack another shell into the chamber and it bucks in my hand with a deafening roar. Derek is standing just to the left of the propane tanks and I know I'm safe from hitting one of them as a black hole appears at the top of his nose and his brains explode out onto the wall behind him.

The sound of the shot leaves a ringing in my ears and the ringing is accentuated by Katie who has just begun screaming in the doorway. Derek's lifeless body slumps to the ground, the shotgun clattering away as he falls. I move to pursue Katie who is running now.

She dashes down the hallway and I'm close behind. I consider shooting her but can't risk her dying. Not yet. She's nearly at the door when I tackle her to the ground. Her fingernails tear deep gouges down the right side of my face but miss my eye. She reaches back for another slash but my own hand is already moving, bringing the revolver around, the heavy frame crashing into the side of her head.

There is a loud impact as the blow connects but nothing crunches. Nothing breaks. When I look down at her, I see that her eyes are closed. Good. She'll be out for a bit, which will make what I have to do much easier.

10

———

The rest of the night passes in a blur.

The first thing I do is tie up Katie's arms and legs. Then I tie her to the chair I've sat in so many times, speaking with Alexis. I make sure that the rope around her wrists and ankles are independent of the ones around the chair so I can cut the chair ones later without risking her getting loose.

Next, I go through her pockets. There is a black rectangle made of glass that I don't recognize, some coins, a small folding knife, and a pair of nail clippers. I remove everything and place it in a small pile on the counter at the opposite end of the room.

Stepping back, I make sure there is nothing even remotely within reach that she can get her hands on. No knives or guns or sharp edges or even blankets or pillows. The room is tight but I manage to make just enough space around her so that she won't be able to get at anything without banging the chair across the wood floor a few times.

With Katie secured, I turn my attention to Derek. When

I re-enter the bedroom, I see that a good deal of blood has leaked out of the massive hole in the back of his head. Frowning, I walk around behind him and hoist him up with my arms wrapped tightly around his chest.

Now it's just a matter of getting him to the door. His hiking boots make a light scraping sound against the smooth floor as I drag him. Once I reach the front door, I hold him up with one arm as I fumble with the locks. It takes a few moments but eventually, the hinges squeal lightly and the cool night air rushes in.

I try to think of something poetic to say. Some sign of respect for the life I have just reluctantly taken. All I can manage though is a "Sorry bud," before I hurl his bulky frame out in front of the house.

The doors aren't even fully locked before I begin to hear wet slurping sounds coming from outside.

ABOUT A HALF-HOUR LATER, I find myself pacing. At some point, I picked up the bottle of whiskey and when I go to pour myself another glass, I'm surprised to find a good deal of it gone. I close my eyes and instantly feel the world begin to spin.

Fear floods into me as I realize that I'm drunk. I just killed someone and tied another person to a chair and now I'm drunk. Stupid. This is the kind of shit Alexis was hoping for.

I set the glass down and hobble off to bed.

THE LIGHT of the next morning screams into my head like a hot knife. Something is banging in the background and I slowly sit up and rub my eyes. It takes a moment for the events of the previous night to come flooding back to me.

Then I'm up and moving, running towards the living room in my long johns.

By the time I get there, Katie is almost within reaching distance of the first aid kit that I failed to hide the night before. I don't know everything that's inside of it but I'd be willing to bet there's some sort of sharp edge she was planning on using to free herself.

Granted, she'd have had to free her hands first or maybe tip the chair and throw herself down onto the floor so she could slowly inch over to the kit and access it with her bound fingers. But I still feel stupid for getting drunk and almost allowing all this to happen.

I boot the kit across the room and it bounces off the wall in the kitchen and comes to rest in the middle of the floor.

"What the fuck are you doing, Walter?" Her voice is angrier than I've ever heard it, as if the indignity of being tied up is worse than what I might do to her. What I'm planning to do to her.

I sit down in one of the wooden chairs and assess her.

"I'm sorry," I say. "I truly am."

She just shakes her head. I can see that she's trying to think of something that might make me come to my senses. But I'm already there. I feel like I haven't thought with this much clarity in a very long time.

"What are you going to do?" she asks.

"You'll see."

She thinks about what that might mean for a second. And then she begins to cry.

"I have a *life* back home," she sobs. "A mother and father who will want to know where I am."

She sees my face falter somewhat. I try to adopt a neutral expression but it's too late.

"What would your daughter think if she was alive?" She continues. "Is this really what she would want?"

"She is alive. You've seen her."

"You know that's not her, Walter. You *know* it. There's nothing you can do to bring her back."

"Derek said it best. He said that there must be some part of her that still wants her father. That's why she's trying so hard to get at me. It's not just survival. It's more than that."

Katie hangs her head. I see the tears and snot running down her face. She tries to wipe them on her shoulder but can't quite manage it. I walk over to the counter and grab a towel but when I try to help her she tries to bite my hand and then spits at me.

"Don't fucking touch me," she snarls.

"Keep it up," I say. "It's much easier to sacrifice a human when they're acting like an animal."

"*I'm sorry, I'm sorry, I'm sorry.*" The turn is almost jarring. From hissing beast to uncontrollable sobbing.

Walking over to the window, I pull back the curtain and look out. Not quite noon yet. We still have a lot of time.

I SPEND the afternoon cleaning up the bodies.

When I go outside, I see that Derek's body has been drained of every last drop of blood. It looks even more destroyed than Wes's, who I find near the edge of the woods where Alexis dropped him.

She's growing stronger, I think to myself. *She hasn't fed this well for years.*

It takes a very long time to dig the three graves. I consider doing a fourth for Katie but then I remember that none of the children's bodies were ever found. The beasts must have had some lair that they brought them back to.

This might be different though. When my father spoke of the old gods that used to inhabit these woods, he referred to them almost as if they were some sort of society. Not like ours. Simpler, yet more divine.

Alexis on the other hand has no society. No elders to show her the way. I have no idea how much time she spent with the other beasts before they died but it could only have been a maximum of a few years. Who knows if she abides by whatever previous feeding traditions they had established?

As I work, I make sure to check frequently on Katie, even giving her something to eat at one point, which she refuses. Oh well, she ended up eating a pretty decent amount of our meal last night after the conversation got going so she should still have quite a bit of nutrients in her.

When I think about our time last night, I wonder if I was planning this even then. A big meal to fatten up the guests. Hansel and Gretel in the cage while the witch feeds them everything they could possibly want.

Two hours before sunset, I cut the rope that binds Katie to the chair. She makes a haphazard lunge for the door but forgets that her feet are tied together and topples to the floor. Unfortunately, I have to cut those ropes too if we're going to walk with any kind of speed.

When I go to free her legs, however, she starts trying to kick me.

"Stop," I say.

She doesn't listen so I get back up and boot her as hard

as I can in the stomach. The wind thoroughly knocked out of her, I lower myself to her face and speak quietly.

"Please don't resist. If you do, I'll just shoot you. She can still drink if you're dead. We already proved that with Derek. I just don't think she prefers it."

She lies there gasping, trying to catch her breath. She looks like a fish. A fish on the ice with its throat cut. Something rises in the back of my throat.

I stand up quickly and slap the side of my face a few times, then blow out a big breath of air. I wring my hands for a few moments.

Once I feel myself beginning to relax again, I drop back down to one knee.

"Are you going to behave?"

She nods, almost imperceptibly.

"Do I have to shoot you?" I place the muzzle of the barrel to her head and her face scrunches up.

"No," she cries. "I'll behave."

"Good. Just remember, I can change my mind at any point so it's in your best interest to be on your best behavior. Who knows, maybe you'll even be able to escape once I leave. Probably not but your chances are better than zero. Better than dying right now."

She nods again and I help her to her feet. Her knees are shaking.

"Now try to walk at a decent pace," I say. "We've got a ways to go and remember, *I* have to walk all the way back."

THE WALK to the clearing is not what I thought it would be. But it's what I should have expected.

Even though Katie is tied up. Even though she knows what's coming and there's no trust being broken here. Even though I have a gun trained at the center of her back. The process is too familiar. So familiar, in fact, I have to stop a couple of times.

The second time I tell Katie to wait, she turns to me and says, "You don't look so good." Then, "Bad memories?"

I don't respond. I just wave the gun at her.

"You think you've had some breakthrough, Walter. But you haven't." Her voice is soft. A delicate blend of compassion and menace. "You think you're doing this for her but you're not. Can't you see that you've felt so guilty for so long that now you're just trying to bury it? Well, let me tell you: there's a big difference between burying what you did and atoning for it."

"There is no atoning," I snap, the words surprising even me. I try to catch my breath but I can't. I feel like I'm at the edge of some cliff, trying to give myself the confidence to jump. "There's nothing I can do to atone for it. This is my only way forward."

"No it's not," she says gently.

"Then what is there?" The question comes out as a shout. Whatever confidence I had in the morning is gone now with the effects of the liquor. Whatever lie I may have told myself is now laid bare to the sun.

"You can let me go. Can't you see this is your second chance? A chance to succeed where you failed before?"

The images reel through my head again. Burning children. My father's words. Tina hanging. Dead fish. Dead bird. Alexis drifting away. Teeth. Nails. Blood. Flesh. Alexis as a grown woman. Strong. So strong now. Better than her father or mother could have ever been. Leaving town to start her own life. Make her own family. Her own children.

"*No!*" I scream. "*She has to live. I have to help her. Have to make her strong!*"

The revolver bucks in my hand and Katie screams as her left knee explodes. She collapses to the ground.

"*You're nothing,*" I scream. "*You're an animal!*"

Another gunshot. Her other knee. More screaming.

The clearing is close now. I'm not broken. This hasn't broken me. I drag Katie a few hundred meters to the gap in the trees and lash her to one of the towering pines and consider putting the gun in her mouth and pulling the trigger but I don't. Then I consider putting the gun in my own mouth but I don't do that either because I'm not fucking broken. This hasn't fucking broken me and I need to keep it together. I need to stay strong for Alexis.

And I'm not broken.

Not yet.

Not until I start walking back.

It's utterly unthinkable that I make it back home before the sun sets but I do. Maybe it's because I'm so preoccupied with my thoughts that my legs just disconnect from my mind and do their own thing. They walk the path I've walked many times before. In my dreams. In my nightmares. The path that I walked on that fateful day and so many days following as I began the slow slide into masochistic, self-loathing destruction.

It's not until I hear Katie's scream off in the distance that I can finally admit to my own regret. Regret for what I've done to her. Done to her friends. My regret for everything.

The door isn't even closed when I put the bottle to my lips. Sweet amber oblivion take me and absolve me with your blissful nothingness. I wonder if it is another lie. Nothingness after death. Whenever I heard my mother-in-law speak about the afterlife I would think that it was just wishful thinking. Something to comfort the people frightened of their own mortality.

Now I see that the eternal sleep is the comfort. Nothingness after death is the thing that soothes you because if there is an afterlife I want no part of it. And I can't believe it wants any part of me.

I walk from room to room, soaking in the memories of a life that has been nothing but one long descent into Hell. It's only once I'm back in the living room that I realize I've been holding the bottle of whiskey sideways and now it's completely empty. I whip it at the window I sat by for the last few decades and both it and the glass pane shatter, the short curtain rod falling down moments after to reveal the dark night outside.

"Come inside," I yell. *"Come get me! I'm here! You're welcome in!"*

The finality of the words settles into me. More final even than Katie's scream. The thought almost sobers me. Almost. I'm glad it doesn't.

My thoughts go to the propane in my room, then to the shotguns, then to my own rifle. I go near none of them. Instead, I walk to the end of the hallway and stick my hands in my pocket. The door to the outside is still cracked open. I put my back against the wall and then slump slowly down to the floor, staring out.

This is it, I think. *After all of these years, she finally has me. Her plan worked.*

The door to my bedroom is open as well and I have a clear line of sight to the stacks of propane. I could walk over and unscrew a bunch of the nozzles. Light a match when she comes in and blow us sky-high. But I don't. I have to see her. I have to talk to her one more time.

I pull my revolver out and check the cylinder. Three bullets left. I don't know what I plan on doing with them. Maybe the propane is still in my mind but I have to remind myself that shooting a metal tank like that won't make it explode. It'll just put a hole in it.

Maybe it's for Alexis. One last shot to the temple as she drains me. One last attempt to put her down. Maybe Alexis, the real Alexis, can finally rest in peace then.

Maybe it's for me. Maybe it always has been.

The hinges to the front door creak and there she is. She looks normal, standing there in her white coat. Just like the day I left her. The image cuts through my heart like a scythe.

"Come in," I say.

She takes a hesitant step inside. She doesn't burst into flame.

I half-expect her to fly at me now that she has me. To turn into her monstrous self. Her true self. But she doesn't. Instead, she just walks slowly over and sits down next to me.

"Hi, papa."

"Hi, sw—Hi, sweetie." The words catch in my throat.

"You let me inside."

I nod.

"It's warm in here," she says. "I've been cold for so long."

"Me too, honey." I feel tears stinging my eyes. "Me too."

"You have a gun."

I nod.

"It won't work."

I nod.

"The winter's going to be long."

I nod.

"Why aren't you talking?"

"It's hard, sweetie. I'm sorry."

"It's okay. I appreciated the present you left for me today."

I don't nod this time. Instead, I just say nothing.

She seems to relax. She knows she has me.

"I've been lonely for a very long time."

"Me too."

"I know you have, papa. Are you ready to join me?"

I notice that she says, "Join me." Not, "Join me and mama." My heart leaps inside of my chest as I realize what she might be talking about.

"Do you mean...are you going to make me like you?"

"Of course, papa. That's why I wanted those people here. I knew that once you were with them, you'd realize how much you actually miss being around people. But I also knew that you'd realize you'd never be accepted by them. Not after everything."

"So, you did this for me?" I feel the tears run down my face. "You want me to be with you? Forever?"

She nods, a big smile on her face.

My mind flashes back to the smile she was wearing after she killed Sarah. I try to push it down.

"I don't know if I can."

"I know," she says. "I wasn't sure it would work out. I thought you might be disgusted with me." She makes the face she made as a child whenever she was embarrassed about something. "I think...you might still be disgusted with me..."

"Never," I say, shaking my head. "Don't you ever think that."

"The elders showed me how to do it. How to turn someone. They always told me that the most important thing is our bloodline. Our family. Even now I can still feel the urge deep down in my tummy. It wants to expand. It wants us to live. I want you to be a part of that, papa. Like you did for me when you and mama made me." She smiles.

"I don't know if I'm ready."

"You don't have to do anything," she says. "Just sit back."

I lean against the wall, watching her. Alexis slowly pulls

the sleeve of her coat down, then lifts her bare wrist to her mouth. She bites down and a thin line of ruby-red blood runs down her arm. She holds it out to me.

"Drink," she says, an expectant look on her face.

I hesitate. I wonder what it will be like. What this afterlife has in store for me. Will it bring with it all the guilt from the past life? Will seeing Alexis in my new form be like seeing her before she died? I don't know and I don't trust her to tell me the truth about it.

Once again, I feel like I'm at the edge of a cliff. I close my eyes and think about it. Then I jump.

The blood tastes sweeter than anything I've ever tasted. If the liquor I had earlier is a drop of oblivion then this is an ocean. It's intoxicating. Absolving. I feel my guilt begin to melt away.

I pull my mouth away and then she crawls up to me, placing her lips to my neck.

"*We'll be together soon,*" she whispers. "*And it'll be forever.*"

I think about what it means to feel this forever. To never feel guilty again. For my great transgressions to be nothing more than tiny steps on the path to salvation.

Is that you? Something whispers in the back of my head. *Is that what you want? To forget?*

The images flash through my head for a final time. So fast that I can't even focus on them. Memories. Memories burning up. Bad memories. Horrible memories. My memories.

I think about the past. About what the future could hold. I think about what's happening right now at this very moment. Where I am. Who I'm with.

What I'm with.

"*I love you sweetie.*" I don't know if I whisper the words or just think them. I feel the grip of the revolver in my hand. I lift the gun off the floor but just barely. I think about all the decisions I've made in my life and how they all turned out to be wrong. I hope that if this is the last one I make, that it's finally the right one.

I pull the trigger and three things happen all at once. First, there is a pain in my wrist as the gun recoils against it at an awkward angle. Second, a tight hole appears in the side of one of the propane tanks and the gas inside immediately begins hissing out. Third, the long trail of alcohol I accidentally poured out earlier is ignited next to me where the fumes reach the detonation of the gunpowder.

Alexis continues to suck at my neck as the fire races over the ground. It goes into the living room, the kitchen, the spare bedroom, the storage room, and most importantly my room.

Nothing else happens for a moment and I feel myself beginning to slip into unconsciousness. Whatever Alexis is doing to me is working. I fight to hold onto the guilt. The pain. The damning images. If this is judgment, then let it claim me.

When the hissing propane finally ignites and the cabin is engulfed in a ball of flame, the last picture in my mind is Alexis. Her face is sad and uncertain. She's standing on a sheet of ice, drifting out into open water.

Paul Fletcher circles Big Lake Harriet once before making his approach. Of all the stops Paul makes in a year, he likes this one the least. He doesn't know much about the town, only that his father was wary of it when this was his route and that he urged Paul to do the same when he took over.

It's July and the days are about as long as they're going to get up here but still, after a few delays on the runway, Paul finds himself touching down on the choppy water of the lake just a bit before sunset. It sets his teeth on edge.

Still, this is a lucrative stop. Walter always has something of value, whether it's pelts or trinkets or even old coins that Paul suspects the man has been stealing from his neighbors.

Is it stealing if the neighbors are dead? He wonders. And they almost certainly are dead. He basically told him as much. Either that or they all decided to pack up and leave one year, with no one but Walter to stay behind.

Maybe Walter killed them, he thinks. If he killed them then it's probably still stealing.

Just so long as he doesn't kill me.

Paul figures the chances of that are extremely low. He's seen how Walter lives out here. He knows that he's the hermit's last lifeline to the world. If Walter did kill him then where would he get his clothes, oil, and propane?

The water would normally be a little rough for the Cessna 185 but Paul has the plane weighed down to the point where it slices through the choppy waves like a knife. He's removed the four rear seats to make room for more cargo and just recently attached a cargo pod to the underbelly of the aircraft. Business is booming as more and more people leave the cities for secluded areas and they need their supplies.

Paul is happy to oblige. For a handsome fee, of course.

Once he's pulled up to the dock, he lashes the floats to the side and bounces the craft lightly in the water with his foot to make sure the buoys do an adequate job of keeping the dock from scratching the paint. Satisfied, he turns and looks into the woods.

It's certainly darker than he would like it to be but he can still see the sun above the horizon, so he's got time. Does he have enough time to go walking into town though to try and find Walter? Shit, what if Walter's dead?

Paul knows it'll happen someday and when it does, he'll probably be the first person to know. He imagines himself walking into the man's house. He's been there a few times and it's larger than one might expect. He doesn't cherish the idea of having to search the rooms to see if he can find the half-decomposed corpse of the last member of this dead community.

Some ways off, a scream splits the air. Paul freezes, listening. Whoever it is, it definitely sounds like a woman. Maybe even a girl. He's not sure.

He hears it again, and this time he can make out a long, drawn-out, "*Help!*"

Paul considers leaving. Thinks about getting back into his plane and flying away. But he's not going to do that. He knows he's not. If he were to high-tail it out of here without investigating, it would gnaw at him forever. He'd be checking the papers to see if there was a serial killer loose in the area or if some hikers had gotten lost or something.

Hikers were always getting lost. Stupid hikers.

Well, if one of them was stuck in a hole with a broken ankle or something and Paul helped her out, then she'd basically be required to sing his praises to the news media. His name and the name of his business would be plastered on every paper in the whole province.

Paul starts walking.

Once on the main trail that leads from the boat landing, Paul has to stop and wait for another scream. When it doesn't come, he yells himself.

"*Hello. Is someone there?*"

"*Hello-o?*" Whoever is yelling stretches the word into three syllables, then, "Can somebody help me? I'm trapped in here."

Whoever is calling out to him is close but they sound like they're inside of something. Maybe a small outbuilding or maybe they're trapped under a canoe or something. He doesn't know.

He calls back and forth with the person a few times, honing in on her position until he comes to a small latrine. The tiny structure is familiar to him as he's used it on a number of occasions after landing. Without any reservation, he yanks the door open.

The place is dark and gloomy, a filmy golden light streaming in through the smudged window cut into the side. As he squints and his eyes adjust, he slowly makes out a figure. Backed into the corner by the toilet. She steps hesitantly into the window's feeble light.

It's a woman. Dark hair and rail thin. God, it feels like he could accidentally break her just by glancing at her wrong. Her clothes are sodden and her face is smudged. Then he notices something weird.

The woman has holes in her jeans, right where the knees are. But they're not the normal kind of holes that you'd see in someone who might be wearing an old and tattered pair. No, these are little holes about the size of a nickel that reveal the pale skin underneath.

He's seen holes like that. Back during his time flying helicopter for the coast guard. Apparently, a big drug exchange had gone south and seven people ended up with a bunch of holes in their clothes that looked remarkably like these two. Except it wasn't skin underneath. It was blood and ragged flesh.

What was more, the fabric of the pants seemed stained around the knees. Not a good sign.

"Are you okay?" Paul asks. He's not totally unnerved yet. The bullet holes are more of a curiosity than anything. But the longer he stands there, the longer something deep inside of his lizard brain tells him to get out.

"He locked me in here," she says.

"Who did?"

"Walter."

"Walter did this?" Paul asks. He's shocked, then he remembers that he opened the door with no problem at all.

It suddenly occurs to him that the girl might be some sort of bait. Maybe Walter is planning to trap him in here for some reason. Paul still has the door propped open slightly with his foot to let a little bit of the evening light in but someone could easily rush him from behind and slam the door on him. From there, it wouldn't take much more than a couple of boards and nails to lock him inside.

He turns around to see if anyone is coming. And that's when he feels something like a vice-grip clamp down on the side of his neck.

Paul screams and stumbles over, the door clapping shut. He's on the ground and now something is ripping at his throat. He furiously tries to slap whatever it is away but red-hot pain lances through his hands as if he has just slapped the business end of a couple of kitchen knives.

Then, something grabs his wrist and in a single twisting motion, he feels his elbow torqued around in a full circle until the ligaments snap. He screams louder but realizes that he's not making much noise beyond a gurgle.

That's when he realizes that he can't breathe. He keeps trying to suck air in but nothing's coming. All there is is a hideous pressure at his neck that grows more intense with every passing second. And as he lies there on the ground, he notices that the dark little latrine is growing darker. The light from the dirty window fades and fades until eventually, it's eclipsed entirely.

———

KATIE FEELS as if the sun itself has just been born inside her chest. She feels power that she hasn't felt since that first day she awoke in the cave, the bones of thousands piled around her. That night she made her first kill. A fat owl on a tree branch.

She remembers falling on it as silently as the falling

snow. Remembers those first couple gulps of hot animal blood. It made her feel like she could do anything. Go anywhere. Kill anyone. And even that feeling is nothing compared to this. This is a human's blood. This is what she was made for.

The winter was long. Walter and Alexis were already dead by the time she woke up. From there, it was all she could do to survive on what little animals remained in the forest. Badgers, squirrels, deer, grouse, even the damn mice. She ate all of them.

By the time spring came around, a few of the migratory birds returned and she plucked them from the sky like fat ripe apples off of a tree. She was starving by then and ate more than she should have, faster than she should have.

When summer arrived, she was in worse shape than she had been four months ago. She was weaker. Slower. What little food remained began evading her. Over the next two months, she withered down to almost nothing.

Then, the pilot.

Katie knew he was coming. Had remembered it from before, speaking with Walter. That's how she sees her life now. Now and before. She's not sure if she likes this better. In fact, she's not sure if she even knows what it is to enjoy something beyond food. All she knows is hunger and satiation.

And right now, she is satiated.

She cannot *believe* the old ones who sired Alexis only took one child a year. The control that must have required. Then again, she can't imagine feeling like this all year round. She feels manic. If the blood of a deer is like caffeine in her system then the blood of a human is like cocaine.

While she has a hard time understanding the rules and rituals the old ones lived by in the preceding centuries, she definitely understands why they would eventually break them. As hungry as she is, she feels as if she could massacre a whole city and drink blood by the river-full, given the oppurtunity.

She thinks of Alexis draining not one but three people before she died. How amazing that must have been. How intoxicating. And that didn't even count the blood she had consumed from Katie.

Katie finds herself mourning Alexis from time to time. Mourning her the way one might mourn a mother she never knew. That day in the clearing, Alexis had told her of how she planned to turn Walter. How she loved him, even now. But she also explained that she lacked faith in him. He was old. Tired. She thought it was possible that he would kill himself before she could reach him.

If that were true, she needed a progeny. Walter could end up killing her, she said. He *had,* in fact, killed her. Or at least, that's the way it looked to Katie when she found the smoking ash heap of his house.

So now, she is the last. A final gamble by a dead species. But she doesn't have to be.

Katie is stronger now than she has ever been. She considered leaving before to find better hunting grounds but never had the strength. Now she does.

Thinking about where to go, Katie suddenly feels a pull deep down inside of her. It's a new sensation. Almost like what sorrow felt like in her old life but it's somehow different. A sort of longing.

Faces swim up into her mind. Faces she hasn't considered since she was turned. Her human mother and father. Her big sister. She knows where they live. She knows that they're probably worried about her.

I have to see them, she thinks. She doesn't know exactly

what she's going to do when she does and she doesn't think about it. In fact, she barely thinks about anything these days. There is just the pull.

The sun has set now. Soon, it will be safe. Safe to leave this town. This forest. Safe to leave everything and start something new. It will take a full night to get to where she needs to go. Maybe two. She doesn't know how much ground she can cover while flying.

But she's ready to find out.

THE END

The Omen Tree

Crimes of the Blood Cults

ABOUT THE AUTHOR

Fredrick Niles is the author of *Ash Above, Snow Below* and *The Omen Tree*. He lives in St. Paul, Minnesota where he writes fiction and plays music. In his free time he rants about movies, lurks in bookstores, and practices introversion with his wife.

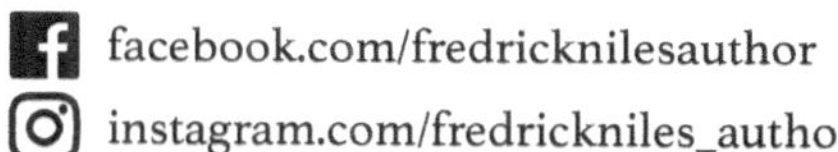

facebook.com/fredricknilesauthor
instagram.com/fredrickniles_author